A SAM & FRIENDS MYSTERY

WITHDRAWN

BOOK FOUR

Witches' Brew

MARY LABATT • JO RIOUX

KIDS CAN PRESS

Kids Can Press acknowledges the financial support of the Government of Ontario, through the Ontario Media Development Corporation's Ontario Book Initiative; the Ontario Arts Council; the Canada Council for the Arts; and the Government of Canada, through the BPIDP, for our publishing activity.

Published in Canada by
Kids Can Press Ltd.
25 Dockside Drive
Toronto, ON M5A 0B5

Published in the U.S. by
Kids Can Press Ltd.
2250 Military Road
Tonawanda, NY 14150

www.kidscanpress.com

Based on the book *Strange Neighbors* by Mary Labatt

Edited by Karen Li
Designed by Kathleen Gray and Rachel Di Salle

CM 11 0 9 8 7 6 5 4 3 2 1
CM PA 11 0 9 8 7 6 5 4 3 2 1

The hardcover edition of this book is smyth sewn casebound.
The paperback edition of this book is limp sewn with a drawn-on cover.
Manufactured in Buji, Shenzhen, China, in 10/2010 by WKT Company

Library and Archives Canada Cataloguing in Publication

Labatt, Mary, 1944–
Witches' brew / written by Mary Labatt ; illustrated by Jo Rioux.

(A Sam & friends mystery ; bk. 4)
ISBN 978-1-55453-472-2 (bound). ISBN 978-1-55453-473-9 (pbk.)

I. Rioux, Jo-Anne II. Title. III. Series: Labatt, Mary, 1944– . Sam & friends mystery ; bk. 4.

PS8573.A135W57 2011   jC813'.54   C2010-904764-8

Kids Can Press is a *Corus*™ Entertainment company

To my family — M.L.

To all my friends — J.R.

We have new neighbors.

Mom and Dad say they rented the house in a hurry. They didn't even look at it first!

That sounds ... mysterious.

CRASH!

Yikes!

That's odd! They've been trained to hop in line.

MREEAOOOW!!!

Sorry, baby! Mama didn't mean to ignore you.

Baby!

Come to mama, darling!

How many mamas does that ugly thing have?

I'm so glad they can't hear you!

The next day ...

Hmm, mad scientists ... I bet those toads used to be people!

Those women didn't look like mad scientists, Sam.

Then it must be a magic spell ... Maybe the toads are waiting for a princess to kiss them ...

Sam thinks it might be magic. Like princesses and witches and stuff.

Witches use toads in their potions!

Witches?

No one else would need toads. Only witches.

Witches would be good. I wonder who they came to put a spell on.

They didn't come to put a spell on anybody, Sam! They're *not* witches! Don't get us into trouble!

It makes me crazy when you and Sam talk. I wish I could hear her.

So do I. Then *you* could argue with her.

Jennie, who else but witches would have toads?

And now we know why they rented the house so fast!

They don't care about the house. They just need a place to cast their spells!

The next day ...

I hate cats.
Almost as much as
I hate teenagers.

SLAM!

Beth!

I got these from the library. They're all about witches.

I hate reading. Just find the facts.

This says witches can be men or women.

Everyone knows that.

A group of witches is called a coven.

They meet four times a year to make plans.

Big deal.

It also says that one of the first signs that witches are casting spells is weird weather.

Weather?

"Casting spells causes huge weather disturbances."

Perfect! Let's find out how they brew their spells! Let's watch —

Sam, I think we should stay away.

Those witches must be casting a spell.

Maybe they're putting a hex on the town.

Maybe they'll turn us all into toads!

I don't want to be a toad, Sam! I like being a person!

I hope that's not what they're doing. I would hate to be a toad.

The next night ...

Jennie?

M-may I take Sam for a walk?

What's the matter? You're white as a ghost.

I can't tell you now. Look!

We're going to Beth's house. I've already called her.

We can go to my room.

Something terrible has happened!

So tell me!

Noel has football practice every day this month ...

Nothing worked. I have to go on Monday.

I know! Ask Beth's mom to babysit!

Could I come to your house instead, Beth?

I already asked. Mom's taking the twins to swimming lessons. I have to go with them.

The next day ...

knock knock

Jennie! You've brought your little friends!

The more the merrier, I always say.

HISSS!

WOOF

Oh! Hello, Sam ...

She doesn't want me to see what they put in their potions!

Later that week ...

Ask them where their animals go.

Where did your parrot go? And the lizard?

Well ... you might say they moved on.

I know where they went! They've eaten them!

Rrring! Rrring!

I'll get it!

Sam says they're eating those animals!

I hope your mom comes soon!

Jennie, your mother has to stay late at the drugstore. So you'll eat supper with us.

Dinner's in the oven.

They've cooked the lizard! One day he's living his life. The next — presto! He's dinner!

I-I'm sick! I have to go home!

You can't go home. Dinner is ready.

43

My appetite is ruined forever.

It was delicious. But ...

But we had a big lunch! A huge lunch! We're still full.

Well it was nice of you to give them dinner. I hope they weren't any trouble.

No trouble at all. They can stay for dinner any time. We have many more secret recipes.

That weekend ...

I love sleepovers!

I made cupcakes, and for Sam ... oatmeal jelly bean cookies!

Great! Get some hot salsa, and life will be perfect.

This looks a lot better than the stuff they eat next door.

I can't stop thinking about that poor lizard.

And how many other animals are missing?

How many animals have disappeared, Beth?

The parrot, the snake, that ugly rat ...

... And the lizard that went into the pie. That's four animals in a week.

Those witches must be boiling them into potions.

They probably make pickles out of their little toes!

Hey! They have a visitor!

Yikes! Another witch!

Get down! Sam thinks he's a witch!

Remember that witch book? He's come for that meeting!

Sam says he's come for the witches' meeting.

Tell us what you see, Sam.

Later that afternoon ...

There they go with another animal!

Let's follow them. Maybe I'll find a way to break this spell.

Sam wants to follow them!

Good idea, Sam! Come on, Jennie!

They're heading toward Main Street.

They're going in there.

It's a pet store.

Here they come!

I know what they're doing! They're turning people into pets — and then selling them!

Sam thinks the witches are turning people into pets and selling them at the pet store.

Let's check it out!

59

Say, guys, do you remember being humans before you were puppies? Think hard.

What's Sam doing?

She's trying to find out if they used to be people. But they don't understand.

Puppies are too dumb.

Sam says it's no use. Let's go.

It's always good to see you, Harold.

It's the witch! We have to hide you!

Hey! They didn't lock their door.

Why do you care?

I care a lot. I'm going to get their spell book! Come on.

They didn't lock the door. Is that what Sam's talking about?

Sam wants to go in and find the spell book.

creeeaak

Don't waste any time! It's spooky in here.

Let's look upstairs.

I'll look in the first room. You look in the next one.

MREEAOOOW!!!

MREEAOOOW!!!

What was that??

It was that crazy cat!

It doesn't matter. The book's not here. Let's go!

What'll we do?

They'll get us now. We don't have a chance!

I'll think of something. You're lucky I'm so smart.

You got us into this, so you are definitely not smart.

Phooey. Stop insulting me or I won't get us out of here.

There's no way out. And there are three *witches* downstairs!

So we've got a little problem.

Maybe we could go out the window.

It looks high.

That drainpipe goes to the shed. We can climb down.

But we can't leave Sam!

72

Stay there until you hear us talking!

knock! knock!

What are we going to do?

I don't know, but at least they've stopped knocking.

Jennie ... Beth ...

Jennie, dear, your mother called. Noel is making extra deliveries for the drugstore.

We know you're in there ...

These witches are getting on my nerves. They are making wimps out of us. And I hate wimps.

S-Sam is sick of us being scared.

Sam's right. I want to do something.

I have an idea. I think it will make a real splash.

Soon ...

Soon ...

That evening ...

We take in mistreated animals and fatten them up.

Fatten them up?

Before we can find new homes for them, they have to be healthy. That's our job.

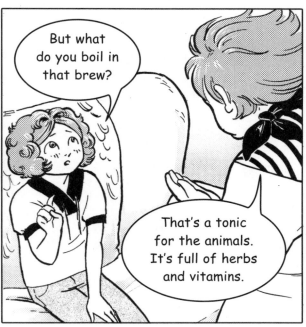

But what do you boil in that brew?

That's a tonic for the animals. It's full of herbs and vitamins.

They don't like it much, but it works!

THE BEST THINGS IN LIFE ARE SPOOKY
Collect all four Sam & Friends Mysteries!

Hardcover 978-1-55453-418-0
Paperback 978-1-55337-303-2

Hardcover 978-1-55337-822-8
Paperback 978-1-55337-302-5

Hardcover 978-1-55453-470-8
Paperback 978-1-55453-471-5

Hardcover 978-1-55453-472-2
Paperback 978-1-55453-473-9